Gratitude Journal

Margaux P. Cloutier

I'm Grateful For...

Start each day with a grateful heart

MONTH:

REASON:

MON

REASON:

TUE

REASON:

WED

REASON:

THU

Grateful Every Day

Thankful, Grateful, Blessed

REASON:

FRI

REASON:

SAT

REASON:

SUN

WEEKLY REFLECTIONS:

Always Stay Grateful

DATE

HOW TO STAY POSITIVE:

HOW I'M FEELING TODAY:

PERSONAL REFLECTIONS:

Daily Affirmations

MORNING:

Daily Affirmation:

Today, I look forward to:

Steps For Success:

THOUGHTS & REFLECTIONS:

Daily Affirmations

AFTERNOON:

I Am Grateful For:

_____

_____

People I am Grateful For:

_____

_____

Blessings In My Life:

_____

_____

EVENING:

Highlights of My Day:

_____

_____

Plans For Tomorrow:

_____

_____

THOUGHTS & REFLECTIONS:

Daily Affirmations

SELF CARE LIST

MON:

TUES:

WED:

THUR:

FRI:

SAT:

SUN:

THIS WEEK'S GOALS:

POSITIVE REMINDERS

HEALTHY HABITS

Reasons To Smile ☺

	I AM GRATEFUL FOR:	WHY:
MONDAY		
TUESDAY		
WEDNESDAY		
THURSDAY		

GRATEFUL THOUGHTS

Reasons To Smile ☺

	I AM GRATEFUL FOR:	WHY:
FRIDAY		
SATURDAY		
SUNDAY		

THIS WEEK I WAS CHALLENGED BY:

FROM THESE CHALLENGES, I LEARNED:

Be Forever Grateful

Be Obsessively Grateful

Be A Magnet for Miracles

Gratitude is the memory of the heart

Gratitude is the best Attitude!

Always be Humble & Kind

Thankful For The Small Things

I'm Grateful For...

Start each day with a grateful heart

MONTH:

REASON:

MON

REASON:

TUE

REASON:

WED

REASON:

THU

Grateful Every Day

Thankful, Grateful, Blessed

REASON:

FRI

REASON:

SAT

REASON:

SUN

WEEKLY REFLECTIONS:

Always Stay Grateful

DATE

_____

HOW TO STAY POSITIVE:

HOW I'M FEELING TODAY:

PERSONAL REFLECTIONS:

Daily Affirmations

MORNING:

Daily Affirmation:

Today, I look forward to:

Steps For Success:

THOUGHTS & REFLECTIONS:

Daily Affirmations

AFTERNOON:

I Am Grateful For:

People I am Grateful For:

Blessings In My Life:

EVENING:

Highlights of My Day:

Plans For Tomorrow:

THOUGHTS & REFLECTIONS:

Daily Affirmations

SELF CARE LIST

MON:

TUES:

WED:

THUR:

FRI:

SAT:

SUN:

THIS WEEK'S GOALS:

POSITIVE REMINDERS

HEALTHY HABITS

Reasons To Smile ☺

	I AM GRATEFUL FOR:	WHY:
MONDAY		
TUESDAY		
WEDNESDAY		
THURSDAY		

GRATEFUL THOUGHTS

Reasons To Smile ☺

	I AM GRATEFUL FOR:	WHY:
FRIDAY		
SATURDAY		
SUNDAY		

THIS WEEK I WAS CHALLENGED BY:

FROM THESE CHALLENGES, I LEARNED:

Be Forever Grateful

Be Obsessively Grateful

Be A Magnet for Miracles

Gratitude is the memory of the heart

Gratitude is the best Attitude!

_____

_____

_____

_____

_____

_____

_____

_____

_____

_____

_____

_____

_____

_____

_____

Always be Humble & Kind

Thankful For The Small Things

I'm Grateful For...

Start each day with a grateful heart

MONTH:

REASON:

MON

REASON:

TUE

REASON:

WED

REASON:

THU

Grateful Every Day

Thankful, Grateful, Blessed

REASON:

FRI

REASON:

SAT

REASON:

SUN

WEEKLY REFLECTIONS:

Always Stay Grateful

DATE

_____

HOW I'M FEELING TODAY:

HOW TO STAY POSITIVE:

PERSONAL REFLECTIONS:

Daily Affirmations

MORNING:

Daily Affirmation:

Today, I look forward to:

Steps For Success:

THOUGHTS & REFLECTIONS:

Daily Affirmations

AFTERNOON:

I Am Grateful For:

People I am Grateful For:

Blessings In My Life:

EVENING:

Highlights of My Day:

Plans For Tomorrow:

THOUGHTS & REFLECTIONS:

Daily Affirmations

SELF CARE LIST

MON:

TUES:

WED:

THUR:

FRI:

SAT:

SUN:

THIS WEEK'S GOALS:

POSITIVE REMINDERS

HEALTHY HABITS

Reasons To Smile ☺

	I AM GRATEFUL FOR:	WHY:
MONDAY		
TUESDAY		
WEDNESDAY		
THURSDAY		

GRATEFUL THOUGHTS

Reasons To Smile ☺

	I AM GRATEFUL FOR:	WHY:
FRIDAY		
SATURDAY		
SUNDAY		

THIS WEEK I WAS CHALLENGED BY:

FROM THESE CHALLENGES, I LEARNED:

Be Forever Grateful

Be Obsessively Grateful

Be A Magnet for Miracles

Gratitude is the memory of the heart

Gratitude is the best Attitude!

_____

_____

_____

_____

_____

_____

_____

_____

_____

_____

_____

_____

_____

_____

_____

Always be Humble & Kind

Thankful For The Small Things

I'm Grateful For...

Start each day with a grateful heart

MONTH:

REASON:

MON

REASON:

TUE

REASON:

WED

REASON:

THU

Grateful Every Day

Thankful, Grateful, Blessed

REASON:

FRI

REASON:

SAT

REASON:

SUN

WEEKLY REFLECTIONS:

Always Stay Grateful

DATE

_____

HOW TO STAY POSITIVE:

HOW I'M FEELING TODAY:

PERSONAL REFLECTIONS:

Daily Affirmations

MORNING:

Daily Affirmation:

_____

_____

_____

Today, I look forward to:

_____

_____

Steps For Success:

_____

_____

THOUGHTS & REFLECTIONS:

Daily Affirmations

AFTERNOON:

I Am Grateful For:

People I am Grateful For:

Blessings In My Life:

EVENING:

Highlights of My Day:

Plans For Tomorrow:

THOUGHTS & REFLECTIONS:

Daily Affirmations

SELF CARE LIST

MON:

TUES:

WED:

THUR:

FRI:

SAT:

SUN:

THIS WEEK'S GOALS:

POSITIVE REMINDERS

HEALTHY HABITS

Reasons To Smile ☺

	I AM GRATEFUL FOR:	WHY:
MONDAY		
TUESDAY		
WEDNESDAY		
THURSDAY		

GRATEFUL THOUGHTS

Reasons To Smile ☺

	I AM GRATEFUL FOR:	WHY:
FRIDAY		
SATURDAY		
SUNDAY		

THIS WEEK I WAS CHALLENGED BY:

FROM THESE CHALLENGES, I LEARNED:

Be Forever Grateful

Be Obsessively Grateful

Be A Magnet for Miracles

Gratitude is the memory of the heart

Gratitude is the best Attitude!

Always be Humble & Kind

Thankful For The Small Things

I'm Grateful For...

Start each day with a grateful heart

MONTH:

REASON:

MON

REASON:

TUE

REASON:

WED

REASON:

THU

Grateful Every Day

Thankful, Grateful, Blessed

REASON:

FRI

REASON:

SAT

REASON:

SUN

WEEKLY REFLECTIONS:

Always Stay Grateful

DATE

_____

HOW TO STAY POSITIVE:

HOW I'M FEELING TODAY:

PERSONAL REFLECTIONS:

Daily Affirmations

MORNING:

Daily Affirmation:

Today, I look forward to:

Steps For Success:

THOUGHTS & REFLECTIONS:

Daily Affirmations

AFTERNOON:

I Am Grateful For:

People I am Grateful For:

Blessings In My Life:

EVENING:

Highlights of My Day:

Plans For Tomorrow:

THOUGHTS & REFLECTIONS:

Daily Affirmations

SELF CARE LIST

MON:

TUES:

WED:

THUR:

FRI:

SAT:

SUN:

THIS WEEK'S GOALS:

POSITIVE REMINDERS

HEALTHY HABITS

Reasons To Smile ☺

	I AM GRATEFUL FOR:	WHY:
MONDAY		
TUESDAY		
WEDNESDAY		
THURSDAY		

GRATEFUL THOUGHTS

Reasons To Smile ☺

I AM GRATEFUL FOR: WHY:

FRIDAY

SATURDAY

SUNDAY

THIS WEEK I WAS CHALLENGED BY:

FROM THESE CHALLENGES, I LEARNED:

Be Forever Grateful

Be Obsessively Grateful

Be A Magnet for Miracles

Gratitude is the memory of the heart

Gratitude is the best Attitude!

Always be Humble & Kind

Thankful For The Small Things

I'm Grateful For...

Start each day with a grateful heart

MONTH:

REASON:

MON

REASON:

TUE

REASON:

WED

REASON:

THU

Grateful Every Day

Thankful, Grateful, Blessed

REASON:

FRI

REASON:

SAT

REASON:

SUN

WEEKLY REFLECTIONS:

Always Stay Grateful

DATE

HOW TO STAY POSITIVE:

_____

HOW I'M FEELING TODAY:

PERSONAL REFLECTIONS:

Daily Affirmations

MORNING:

Daily Affirmation:

_____

_____

_____

Today, I look forward to:

_____

_____

_____

Steps For Success:

_____

_____

_____

THOUGHTS & REFLECTIONS:

Daily Affirmations

AFTERNOON:

I Am Grateful For:

People I am Grateful For:

Blessings In My Life:

EVENING:

Highlights of My Day:

Plans For Tomorrow:

THOUGHTS & REFLECTIONS:

Daily Affirmations

SELF CARE LIST

MON:

TUES:

WED:

THUR:

FRI:

SAT:

SUN:

THIS WEEK'S GOALS:

POSITIVE REMINDERS

HEALTHY HABITS

Reasons To Smile ☺

	I AM GRATEFUL FOR:	WHY:
MONDAY		
TUESDAY		
WEDNESDAY		
THURSDAY		

GRATEFUL THOUGHTS

Reasons To Smile ☺

	I AM GRATEFUL FOR:	WHY:
FRIDAY		
SATURDAY		
SUNDAY		

THIS WEEK I WAS CHALLENGED BY:

FROM THESE CHALLENGES, I LEARNED:

Be Forever Grateful

Be Obsessively Grateful

Be A Magnet for Miracles

Gratitude is the memory of the heart

Gratitude is the best Attitude!

Always be Humble & Kind

Thankful For The Small Things

I'm Grateful For...

Start each day with a grateful heart

MONTH:

REASON:

MON

_____

_____

REASON:

TUE

_____

_____

REASON:

WED

_____

_____

REASON:

THU

_____

_____

Grateful Every Day

Thankful, Grateful, Blessed

REASON:

FRI

REASON:

SAT

REASON:

SUN

WEEKLY REFLECTIONS:

Always Stay Grateful

DATE

HOW TO STAY POSITIVE:

HOW I'M FEELING TODAY:

PERSONAL REFLECTIONS:

Daily Affirmations

MORNING:

Daily Affirmation:

Today, I look forward to:

Steps For Success:

THOUGHTS & REFLECTIONS:

Daily Affirmations

AFTERNOON:

I Am Grateful For:

People I am Grateful For:

Blessings In My Life:

EVENING:

Highlights of My Day:

Plans For Tomorrow:

THOUGHTS & REFLECTIONS:

Daily Affirmations

SELF CARE LIST

MON:

TUES:

WED:

THUR:

FRI:

SAT:

SUN:

HEALTHY HABITS

THIS WEEK'S GOALS:

POSITIVE REMINDERS

Reasons To Smile ☺

	I AM GRATEFUL FOR:	WHY:
MONDAY		
TUESDAY		
WEDNESDAY		
THURSDAY		

GRATEFUL THOUGHTS

Reasons To Smile ☺

	I AM GRATEFUL FOR:	WHY:
FRIDAY		
SATURDAY		
SUNDAY		

THIS WEEK I WAS CHALLENGED BY:

FROM THESE CHALLENGES, I LEARNED:

Made in the USA
Las Vegas, NV
22 June 2021